MOTHER GOOSE

MOTHER GOOSE

More Than 100 Famous Rhymes!

Re-arranged and Edited **in this** *Form by*
EULALIE OSGOOD GROVER

Illustrated by
FREDERICK RICHARDSON

First published in 1919 by Checkerboard Press, Inc.

First Racehorse for Young Readers Edition 2017

All rights to any and all materials in copyright owned by the publisher are strictly reserved by the publisher.

Racehorse for Young Readers books may be purchased in bulk at special discounts for sales promotion, corporate gifts, fund-raising, or educational purposes. Special editions can also be created to specifications. For details, contact the Special Sales Department, Skyhorse Publishing, 307 West 36th Street, 11th Floor, New York, NY 10018 or info@skyhorsepublishing.com.

Racehorse for Young Readers™ is a pending trademark of Skyhorse Publishing, Inc.®, a Delaware corporation.

Visit our website at www.skyhorsepublishing.com.

10 9 8 7 6 5 4 3 2 1

Library of Congress Cataloging-in-Publication Data is available on file.

Print ISBN: 978-1-944686-09-3
Ebook ISBN: 978-1-944686-18-5

Cover and interior artwork by Frederick Richardson

Printed in China

A FOREWORD

Children, as well as their interested parents, will eagerly welcome this beautiful edition of the one great nursery classic, just as a worthy edition of Shakespeare is welcomed by discriminating adult readers.

But some may ask what there is in these simple melodies, attributed to Mother Goose, which gives them so secure and beloved a place in the home, the school and the public library. Is it the humor, the action, the rhythm, or the mystery of the theme which appeals so strongly to critical little minds in each generation of childhood, and even to adult minds so fortunate as to have retained some of the refreshing naiveté of early years?

It is useless to try to explain the charm of these nonsense melodies. The children themselves do not know why they love them. No mother can tell us the magic of the spell which seems to be cast over her restless baby as she croons to it a Mother Goose lullaby. No primary teacher quite understands why the mere repetition or singing of a Mother Goose jingle will transform her listless, inattentive class into one all eagerness and attention. But mother and teacher agree that the best of these verses have an even more potent influence than that of innocently diverting and entertaining the child. The healthy moral, so subtly suggested in many of the rhymes, is unconsciously absorbed by the child's receptive mind, helping him to make his own distinction between right and wrong, bravery and cowardice, generosity and selfishness.

From a literary standpoint, also, these rhymes have proved of real value in creating a taste for the truly musical in poetry and song. They train the ear and stir the imagination of the child as no other verses do. Many famous poets and writers trace their first inspiration, and love for things literary, back to the nursery songs and fairy tales of their childhood.

Teachers well know that children who have reveled in these rhymes and stories, at the time of their strongest appeal, step naturally and appreciatively into the great fields of good literature which are beyond.

Knowing these things to be true, we do not hesitate to place this venerable classic on the shelf beside our Shakespeare, and to send our children there for delight and inspiration. They will understand Shakespeare the better for having known and loved Mother Goose.

But what about the personality of this classic writer? Was she really Mistress Elizabeth Goose who is said to have lived in Boston about two hundred years ago, and who crooned her nonsense jingles to a large and happy family of grandchildren? We are told that their father, Thomas Fleet, who was a printer by trade, thought to turn an honesty penny with his mother-in-law's popular verses, so he published them in a small volume under the title of "Songs for the Nursery: or, Mother Goose's Melodies." A goose with a very long neck and a wide-open mouth flew across the title page, at least so the story goes. But we have to believe that it is only a story, for no copy of the book can be found, and nothing but tradition identifies Elizabeth Goose, the Boston grandmother, with the famous rhymester.

We might feel sorry to be obliged to discredit this picturesque story of Mother Goose, if her real history were not even more mysterious. We know very little about the beloved patron of childhood, but what we do know is as follows:

Mother Goose is most certainly of respectable French origin, for in 1697 a distinguished French writer, Charles Perrault, published in Paris a little book of familiar stories called "Contes de ma Mère l'Oye," or "Tales of My Mother Goose." Her identity, however, he leaves a mystery, except that in the frontispiece of his book is pictured an old woman by her fireside telling stories to an eager little family group.

This volume contained the only prose tales that have ever been credited to Mother Goose, and they are still among the most popular

stories in nursery or school room. The titles are as follows: "Little Red Riding Hood;" "The Sisters Who Dropped From Their Mouths Diamonds and Toads;" "Bluebeard;" "The Sleeping Beauty;" "Puss in Boots;" "Cinderella;" "Riquet With the Tuft;" and "Tom Thumb."

It is through her verses, however, that Mother Goose has won her well-deserved fame. The first collection under her name was published in London about 1765 by John Newbery. It may be, if Oliver Goldsmith were living, he could tell us more about the origin of these verses than we are now ever likely to know. It is more than probable that he himself edited the little volume for John Newbery, and that he wrote the clever preface, "By a very Great Writer of very Little Books," as well as the quaint moral which supplements each rhyme.

About twenty-five years later this book was reprinted in our country by Isaiah Thomas of Worcester, Massachusetts. Several copies of this edition are preserved, one of which has been photographed and reproduced in facsimile by W. H. Whitmore of Boston. Other publishers also reprinted the English edition, one being done for John Newbery's grandson, Francis Power, in 1791.

In 1810 another collection of melodies appeared under the title of "Gammer Gurton's Garland." It was quite evidently a rival of Mother Goose, though it contained nearly all of her verses, besides many far less interesting ones gathered from other sources.

Gammer Gurton's popularity, however, was short, and Mother Goose was revived about 1825 by a Boston firm, Munroe and Francis. Since that time her fame has never waned. In spite of the present multiplicity of beautiful books for children, they are constantly exhausting large editions of the one universally beloved book of melodies. Some of these volumes have been collected and edited by men of the highest literary judgment and ability, such as Goldsmith (with hardly a doubt), Ritson, Halliwell, Andrew Lang, Charles Eliot Norton, Charles Welsh and Edward Everett Hale. Certainly there is not another collection of juvenile literature which can boast such a list of scholarly editors. The deepest gratitude is due them for their careful and discriminating effort to preserve for the children of future generations this rich heritage of nursery melodies.

Many less discriminating editors, however, have ruthlessly mutilated and adapted many of the rhymes to suit their fancy, thinking, possibly, that as Mother Goose is only a title, the verses attributed to her belong to the general public to use as it sees fit. On the contrary, Mother Goose's melodies belong to the children, and no addition or change should be made except by those who are in such close sympathy with the child-heart that they may act with the child's authority.

This present edition of "Mother Goose" preserves the best of the verses which became so popular in England and America as to first demand their publication. It is the only truly classic edition that has been published in modern times. The two authorities which have been followed are the edition published for John Newbery's grandson in London in 1791, and probably edited by Oliver Goldsmith, and the edition published in Boston in 1833 by Munroe and Francis, called "The Only True Mother Goose Melodies." It is from this copy that the following quaint introduction by "Ma'am Goose" is quoted.

Not all the favorites among the nursery rhymes are here, only those that first helped to make the fame of the fictitious but no less worthy patron of childhood. May her fame and her melodies be lovingly preserved to give joy and inspiration to many future generations of little children.

EULALIE OSGOOD GROVER

Hear What Ma'am Goose Says!

My dear little Blossoms, there are now in this world, and always will be, a great many grannies besides myself, both in petticoats and pantaloons, some a deal younger, to be sure, but all monstrous wise and of my own family name. These old women, who never had chick or child of their own, but who always know how to bring up other people's children, will tell you with long faces that my enchanting, quieting, soothing volume, my all-sufficient anodyne for cross, peevish, won't-be-comforted little bairns, ought be laid aside for more learned books, such as *they* could select and publish. Fudge! I tell you that all their batterings can't deface my beauties, nor their wise pratings equal my wiser prattlings; and all imitators of my refreshing songs might as well write another Billy Shakespeare as another Mother Goose—we two great poets were born together, and shall go out of the world together.

No, no, my melodies will never die,
While nurses sing, or babies cry.

*From "The Only True Mother Goose Melodies.
Published by Munroe & Francis, Boston, 1833*

OLD MOTHER GOOSE

Old Mother Goose, when
   She wanted to wander,
Would ride through the air
   On a very fine gander.

Mother Goose had a house,
   'Twas built in a wood,
An owl at the door
   For a porter stood.

She had a son Jack,
   A plain-looking lad,
He was not very good,
   Nor yet very bad.

She sent him to market,
   A live goose he bought:
"Here! mother," says he,
   "It will not go for nought."

Jack's goose and her gander
   Grew very fond;
They'd both eat together,
   Or swim in one pond.

Jack found one morning,
   As I have been told,
His goose had laid him
   An egg of pure gold.

Jack rode to his mother,
   The news for to tell.
She called him a good boy,
   And said it was well.

And Old Mother Goose
   The goose saddled soon,
And mounting its back,
   Flew up to the moon.

Old Mother Goose, when
  She wanted to wander,
Would ride through the air
  On a very fine gander.

Cock-a-doodle-doo,
My dame has lost her shoe:
My master's lost his fiddlestick,
And knows not what to do.

Peter, Peter, pumpkin eater,
Had a wife and couldn't keep her;
He put her in a pumpkin shell,
And then he kept her very well.

Peter, Peter, pumpkin eater,
Had another, and didn't love her;
Peter learned to read and spell,
And then he loved her very well.

Lady-bird, Lady-bird,
Fly away home,
Your house is on fire,
Your children will burn.

One misty, moisty morning,
When cloudy was the weather,
I chanced to meet an old man clothed all in leather.
He began to compliment, and I began to grin,
How do you do, and how do you do?
And how do you do again?

I like little pussy, her coat is so warm,
And if I don't hurt her she'll do me no harm;
So I'll not pull her tail, nor drive her away,
But pussy and I very gently will play.

Little Bo-peep has lost her sheep,
And can't tell where to find them;
Leave them alone, and they'll come home,
And bring their tails behind them.

Little Nanny Etticoat
In a white petticoat,
    And a red nose;
The longer she stands
    The shorter she grows.

Jack, be nimble; Jack, be quick;
Jack, jump over the candlestick.

Pretty John Watts,
We are troubled with rats,
Will you drive them out of the house?
We have mice, too, in plenty,
That feast in the pantry,
But let them stay
And nibble away,
What harm in a little brown mouse?

I'll tell you a story
About Mary Morey,
And now my story's begun.
I'll tell you another
About her brother,
And now my story's done.

Hush-a-bye, Baby, upon the tree top,
When the wind blows the cradle will rock;
When the bough breaks the cradle will fall,
Down tumbles cradle and Baby and all.

Ride away, ride away,
　　Johnny shall ride,
And he shall have pussy-cat
　　Tied to one side;
And he shall have little dog
　　Tied to the other,
And Johnny shall ride
　　To see his grandmother.

Dickery, dickery, dock,
The mouse ran up the clock;
The clock struck one,
The mouse ran down,
Dickery, dickery, dock.

A, B, C, D, E, F, G,
H, I, J, K, L, M, N, O, P,
Q, R, S, and T, U, V,
W, X, and Y and Z.
Now I've said my A, B, C,
Tell me what you think of me.

The little robin grieves
    When the snow is on the ground,
For the trees have no leaves,
    And no berries can be found.

The air is cold, the worms are hid;
    For robin here what can be done?
Let's strow around some crumbs of bread,
    And then he'll live till snow is gone.

Little Tommy Tittlemouse
Lived in a little house;
He caught fishes
In other men's ditches.

About the bush, Willie, about the bee-hive,
About the bush, Willie, I'll meet thee alive.

Bah, bah, black sheep,
    Have you any wool?
Yes, marry, have I,
    Three bags full;
One for my master,
    One for my dame,
But none for the little boy
    Who cries in the lane.

Hickety, pickety, my black hen,
She lays eggs for gentlemen:
Gentlemen come every day
To see what my black hen doth lay.

Willie boy, Willie boy,
   Where are you going?
O, let us go with you
   This sunshiny day.

I'm going to the meadow
   To see them a-mowing,
I'm going to help the girls
   Turn the new hay.

Three children sliding on the ice
    Upon a summer's day,
As it fell out, they all fell in,
    The rest they ran away.

Oh, had these children been at school,
    Or sliding on dry ground,
Ten thousand pounds to one penny
    They had not then been drowned.

Ye parents who have children dear,
    And ye, too, who have none,
If you would keep them safe abroad,
    Pray keep them safe at home.

Wee Willie Winkie runs through the town,
Upstairs and downstairs, in his nightgown;
Tapping at the window, crying at the lock:
"Are the babes in their beds, for it's now ten o'clock?

There was an old woman who lived in a shoe,
She had so many children she didn't know what to do.
She gave them some broth without any bread,
She whipped them all soundly and put them to bed.

There was a man and he had naught,
  And robbers came to rob him;
He crept up to the chimney top,
  And then they thought they had him.
But he got down on the other side,
  And then they could not find him;
He ran fourteen miles in fifteen days,
  And never looked behind him.

There was an old man,
And he had a calf,
And that's half;
He took him out of the stall,
And put him on the wall,
And that's all.

Bow, wow, wow!
Whose dog art thou?
Little Tom Tinker's dog,
Bow, wow, wow!

Pussy-Cat sits by the fire:
 How can she be fair?
In walks the little dog:
 Says: "Pussy, are you there?
How do you do, Mistress Pussy?
 Mistress Pussy, how d'ye do?"
"I thank you kindly, little dog,
 I fare as well as you!"

Here am I, little jumping Joan,
When nobody's with me
        I'm always alone.

There was an old woman lived under the hill,
And if she's not gone she lives there still.
Baked apples she sold, and cranberry pies,
And she's the old woman that never told lies.

Simple Simon met a pieman
    Going to the fair;
Says Simple Simon to the pieman:
  "Pray let me taste your ware."

Says the pieman to Simple Simon:
  "Show me first your penny;"
Says Simple Simon to the pieman:
  "Indeed I have not any."

Sing a song of sixpence, a bag full of rye,
Four and twenty blackbirds baked in a pie;
When the pie was opened the birds began to sing,
And wasn't this a dainty dish to set before the king?
The king was in the parlor counting out his money;
The queen was in the kitchen eating bread and honey;
The maid was in the garden hanging out the clothes,
There came a little blackbird and nipped off her nose.

To market, to market, to buy a fat pig,
Home again, home again, jiggety, jig.

Ride a cock horse
To Banbury Cross
To see what Tommy can buy:
A penny white loaf,
A penny white cake,
And a two-penny apple pie.

Little Miss Muffet
Sat on a tuffet,
Eating some curds and whey;
There came a great spider,
And sat down beside her,
And frightened Miss Muffet away.

Three wise men of Gotham
Went to sea in a bowl,
And if the bowl had been stronger
My song had been longer.

There were two birds sat upon a stone,
    Fal de ral–al de ral–laddy.
One flew away and then there was one,
    Fal de ral–al de ral–laddy.
The other flew after and then there was none,
    Fal de ral–al de ral–laddy.
So the poor stone was left all alone,
    Fal de ral–al de ral–laddy.
One of these little birds back again flew,
    Fal de ral–al de ral–laddy.
The other came after and then there were two,
    Fal de ral–al de ral–laddy.
Says one to the other: "Pray, how do you do?"
    Fal de ral–al de ral–laddy.
"Very well, thank you, and pray how are you?"
    Fal de ral–al de ral–laddy.

Bye, Baby bunting,
Father's gone a-hunting,
Mother's gone a-milking,
Sister's gone a-silking,
And Brother's gone to buy a skin
To wrap the Baby bunting in.

Little Polly Flinders
Sat among the cinders
  Warming her pretty little toes;
Her mother came and caught her,
Whipped her little daughter
  For spoiling her nice new clothes.

Tom, Tom, the piper's son,
Stole a pig, and away he run;
   The pig was eat,
   And Tom was beat,
And Tom ran crying down the street.

Jack and Jill went up the hill
    To fetch a pail of water;
Jack fell down and broke his crown,
    And Jill came tumbling after.

Pussy cat, pussy cat, where have you been?
I've been to London to see the Queen.
Pussy cat, pussy cat, what did you there?
I frightened a little mouse under the chair.

Pat a cake, pat a cake, Baker's man;
So I do, master, as fast as I can.
Pat it and prick it and mark it with T,
And then it will serve for Tommy and me.

Little Boy Blue, come blow your horn,
The sheep's in the meadow, the cow's in the corn.
What! Is this the way you mind your sheep,
Under the haycock fast asleep?

There was an old woman tossed in a blanket
    Seventeen times as high as the moon;
But where she was going no mortal could tell,
    For under her arm she carried a broom.

"Old woman, old woman, old woman," said I,
Whither, ah whither, ah whither so high?"
To sweep the cobwebs from the sky,
And I'll be with you by and by."

Cold and raw the north winds blow
Bleak in the morning early,
All the hills are covered with snow,
And winter's now come fairly.

The man in the moon came down too soon
    To inquire the way to Norridge;
The man in the south, he burnt his mouth
    With eating cold plum porridge.

Four-and-twenty tailors
    Went to kill a snail;
The best man among them
    Durst not touch her tail;
She put out her horns
    Like a little Kyloe cow.
Run, tailors, run, or
    She'll kill you all just now.

Lucy Locket lost her pocket.
Kitty Fisher found it;
There was not a penny in it,
But a ribbon round it.

Little Tom Tucker
Sings for his supper.
What shall he eat?
White bread and butter.
How will he cut it
Without e'er a knife?
How will he marry
Without e'er a wife?

"To bed, to bed," says Sleepy-Head;
 "Let's stay awhile," says Slow;
"Put on the pot," says Greedy-Sot,
 "We'll sup before we go."

Diddle, diddle, dumpling, my son John,
Went to bed with his breeches on,
One stocking off, and one stocking on,
Diddle, diddle, dumpling, my son John.

High diddle diddle,
The cat and the fiddle,
The cow jumped over the moon;
The little dog laughed
To see such craft,
And the dish ran away with the spoon.

The two gray kits,
And the gray kits' mother,
All went over
The bridge together.

The bridge broke down,
They all fell in;
"May the rats go with you,"
Says Tom Bolin.

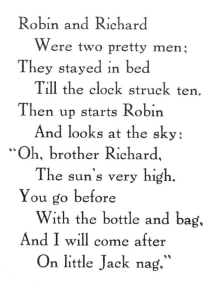

Robin and Richard
    Were two pretty men;
They stayed in bed
    Till the clock struck ten.
Then up starts Robin
    And looks at the sky:
"Oh, brother Richard,
    The sun's very high.
You go before
    With the bottle and bag,
And I will come after
    On little Jack nag."

Is John Smith within?—Yes, that he is.
Can he set a shoe?   Ay, marry, two.
Here a nail and there a nail,
Tick—tack—too.

I had a little hen, the prettiest ever seen,
She washed me the dishes and kept the house clean.
She went to the mill to fetch me some flour,
And always got home in less than an hour.
She baked me my bread, she brewed me my ale,
She sat by the fire and told many a fine tale.

When I was a little boy I lived by myself,
And all the bread and cheese I got I put upon a shelf;
The rats and the mice, they made such a strife,
I was forced to go to London to buy me a wife.
The streets were so broad and the lanes were so narrow,
I was forced to bring my wife home in a wheelbarrow;
The wheelbarrow broke and my wife had a fall,
And down came the wheelbarrow, wife and all.

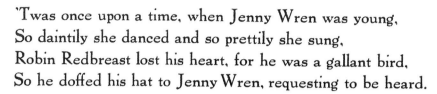

'Twas once upon a time, when Jenny Wren was young,
So daintily she danced and so prettily she sung,
Robin Redbreast lost his heart, for he was a gallant bird,
So he doffed his hat to Jenny Wren, requesting to be heard.

"O, dearest Jenny Wren, if you will but be mine,
You shall feed on cherry pie and drink new currant wine,
I'll dress you like a goldfinch or any peacock gay,
So, dearest Jen, if you'll be mine let us appoint the day."

Jenny blushed behind her fan and thus declared her mind:
"Since, dearest Bob, I love you well, I take your offer kind;
Cherry pie is very nice and so is currant wine,
But I must wear my plain brown gown and never go too fine."

How many days has my baby to play?
    Saturday, Sunday, Monday,
    Tuesday, Wednesday, Thursday, Friday,
    Saturday, Sunday, Monday.

Humpty Dumpty sat on a wall,
Humpty Dumpty had a great fall;
All the king's horses and all the king's men
Couldn't put Humpty Dumpty together again.

Little King Boggen he built a fine hall,
Pie-crust and pastry-crust, that was the wall;
The windows were made of black puddings and white,
And slated with pancakes,—you ne'er saw the like!

As I went to Bonner
  I met a pig
  Without a wig,
Upon my word and honor.

Little Jack Horner
Sat in a corner
Eating a Christmas pie;
He put in his thumb,
And pulled out a plum,
And said: "Oh, what a good boy am I!'

Miss Jane had a bag and a mouse was in it;
She opened the bag, he was out in a minute.
The cat saw him jump and run under the table,
And the dog said: "Catch him, Puss, soon as you're able."

The Queen of Hearts,
She made some tarts
All on a summer's day;
The Knave of Hearts,
He stole those tarts,
And took them clean away.

The King of Hearts
Called for the tarts,
And beat the Knave full sore;
The Knave of Hearts
Brought back the tarts,
And vowed he'd steal no more.

Goosey, goosey, gander, where dost thou wander?
Upstairs and downstairs and in my lady's chamber;
There I met an old man that wouldn't say his prayers,
I took him by his hind legs and threw him downstairs.

See saw, Margery Daw,
    Jacky shall have a new master:
Jacky must have but a penny a day
Because he can work no faster.

Daffy-down-dilly is now come to town
With a petticoat green and a bright yellow gown.

"Cock, cock, cock, cock,
I've laid an egg,
Am I to gang ba-are-foot?"

"Hen, hen, hen, hen,
I've been up and down
To every shop in town,
And cannot find a shoe
To fit your foot,
If I'd crow my hea-art out."

The lion and the unicorn
  Were fighting for the crown.
The lion beat the unicorn
  All about the town.
Some gave them white bread,
  And some gave them brown;
Some gave them plum-cake,
  And sent them out of town.

Old King Cole
Was a merry old soul,
And a merry old soul was he;
He called for his pipe,
And he called for his bowl,
And he called for his fiddlers three.

Mistress Mary, quite contrary,
How does your garden grow?
With silver bells and cockle shells
And pretty maids all in a row.

Bonny lass, pretty lass,
    Wilt thou be mine?
Thou shalt not wash dishes
    Nor yet serve the swine.
Thou shalt sit on a cushion
    And sew a fine seam,
And thou shalt eat strawberries,
    Sugar and cream.

Handy-spandy, Jacky dandy,
Loves plum cake and sugar candy.
He bought some at a grocer's shop,
And pleased away went hop, hop, hop.

Ding–dong–bell, the cat's in the well.
  Who put her in?   Little Johnny Green.
  Who pulled her out?   Great Johnny Stout.
    What a naughty boy was that
    To drown poor pussy cat
  Who never did him any harm,
  And killed the mice in his father's barn.

This pig went to market,
That pig stayed at home;
This pig had roast meat,
That pig had none;
This pig went to the barn door,
And cried "week. week," for more.

There were two blackbirds sitting on a hill,
One named Jack and the other named Jill.
Fly away, Jack!   Fly away, Jill!
Come again, Jack!   Come again, Jill!

Cross patch, draw the latch,
Sit by the fire and spin;
Take a cup and drink it up,
Then call your neighbors in.

Old Mother Hubbard
Went to the cupboard
    To get her poor dog a bone;
But when she came there
The cupboard was bare,
    And so the poor dog had none.

Pease-porridge hot,
    Pease-porridge cold,
Pease-porridge in the pot
    Nine days old.
Spell me that in four letters:
    I will: THAT.

Polly, put the kettle on,
Polly, put the kettle on,
Polly, put the kettle on,
    We'll all have tea.
Sukey, take it off again,
Sukey, take it off again,
Sukey, take it off again,
    They're all gone away.

The sow came in with the saddle,
The little pig rocked the cradle,
The dish jumped up on the table
To see the pot swallow the ladle.
The spit that stood behind the door
Threw the pudding-stick on the floor.
"Odsplut!", said the gridiron,
    "Can't you agree?
I'm the head constable,
    Bring them to me!"

Little Robin Redbreast sat upon a tree,
Up went the Pussy-Cat, and down went he,
Down came Pussy-Cat, away Robin ran;
Says little Robin Redbreast: "Catch me if you can!"

Little Robin Redbreast jumped upon a spade,
Pussy-Cat jumped after him, and then he was afraid.
Little Robin chirped and sang, and what did Pussy say?
Pussy-Cat said: "Mew, mew, mew," and Robin flew away.

A farmer went trotting upon his gray mare,
   Bumpety, bumpety, bump,
With his daughter behind him, so rosy and fair,
   Lumpety, lumpety, lump.

A raven cried "Croak," and they all tumbled down,
   Bumpety, bumpety, bump;
The mare broke her knees and the farmer his crown,
   Lumpety, lumpety, lump.

The mischievous raven flew laughing away,
   Bumpety, bumpety, bump,
And vowed he would serve them the same next day,
   Lumpety, lumpety, lump.

There was an old woman
　　Sold puddings and pies;
She went to the mill,
　　And dust flew in her eyes.
While through the streets,
To all she meets
　　She ever cries:
　　"Hot Pies—Hot Pies."

"Old woman, old woman, shall we go a-shearing?"
"Speak a little louder, sir, I'm very thick o' hearing."
"Old woman, old woman, shall I kiss you dearly?"
"Thank you, kind sir, I hear very clearly."

My little old man and I fell out;
I'll tell you what 'twas all about:
I had money and he had none,
And that's the way the noise begun.

Jack Sprat could eat no fat,
   His wife could eat no lean;
So 'twixt them both they cleared the cloth,
   And licked the platter clean.

There was an old woman, and what do you think?
She lived upon nothing but victuals and drink;
Victuals and drink were the chief of her diet,
And yet this old woman could never be quiet.

What's the news of the day,
Good neighbor, I pray?
They say the balloon
Has gone up to the moon,

There was a crooked man,
　　And he went a crooked mile,
He found a crooked sixpence
　　Against a crooked stile;
He bought a crooked cat
　　Which caught a crooked mouse,
And they all lived together
　　In a little crooked house.

There was a piper had a cow,
 And he had naught to give her;
He pulled out his pipes and played her a tune,
 And bade the cow consider.

The cow considered very well,
 And gave the piper a penny,
And bade him play the other tune,
 "Corn rigs are bonny."

The man in the wilderness
    Asked me
How many strawberries
    Grew in the sea.
I answered him
    As I thought good,
As many red herrings
    As grew in the wood.

Hark! Hark!
The dogs do bark,
The beggars are coming to town;
Some in rags,
Some in tags,
And some in velvet gown.

As I was going to St. Ives
I met seven wives.
Every wife had seven sacks,
Every sack had seven cats,
Every cat had seven kits.
Kits, cats, sacks and wives,
How many were going to St. Ives?

I had a little husband no bigger than my thumb,
I put him in a pint pot, and there I bid him drum;
I bought a little handkerchief to wipe his little nose,
And a pair of little garters to tie his little hose.

Great A, little a,
    Bouncing B;
The cat's in the cupboard,
    And she can't see.

Bat, bat,
  Come under my hat,
And I'll give you a slice of bacon;
  And when I bake
  I'll give you a cake,
If I am not mistaken.

As I was going up Primrose Hill,
    Primrose Hill was dirty;
There I met a pretty lass,
    And she dropped me a curtsey.

Little lass, pretty lass,
    Blessings light upon you;
If I had half-a-crown a day,
    I'd spend it all upon you.

There was a little boy went into a barn
    And lay down on some hay;
A calf came out and smelled about,
    And the little boy ran away.

When good King Arthur ruled his land
    He was a goodly king;
He stole three pecks of barley meal
    To make a bag-pudding.
A bag-pudding the king did make,
    And stuffed it well with plums,
And in it put great lumps of fat
    As big as my two thumbs.
The king and queen did eat thereof,
    And noblemen beside,
And what they could not eat that night
    The queen next morning fried.

"Jacky, come give me your fiddle,
    If ever you mean to thrive."
"Nay, I'll not give my fiddle
    To any man alive.

"If I should give my fiddle
    They'll think that I'm gone mad,
For many a joyful day
    My fiddle and I have had."

One, two, three, four, five,
I caught a hare alive;
Six, seven, eight, nine, ten,
I let him go again.

The north wind doth blow,
And we shall have snow,
And what will poor robin do then?
Poor thing!

He'll sit in the barn
And keep himself warm,
And hide his head under his wing.
Poor thing!

"You owe me five shillings,"
  Say the bells of St. Helen's.

"When will you pay me?"
  Say the bells of Old Bailey.

"When I grow rich,"
  Say the bells of Shoreditch.

"When will that be?"
  Say the bells of Stepney.

"I do not know,"
  Says the great Bell of Bow.

"Two sticks in an apple,"
  Ring the bells of Whitechapel.

"Halfpence and farthings,"
  Say the bells of St. Martin's.

"Kettles and pans,"
  Say the bells of St. Ann's.

"Brickbats and tiles,"
  Say the bells of St. Giles.

"Old shoes and slippers,"
  Say the bells of St. Peter's.

"Pokers and tongs,"
  Say the bells of St. John's.

There was a man in our town,
And he was wondrous wise,
He jumped into a bramble-bush,
And scratched out both his eyes;
And when he saw his eyes were out,
With all his might and main
He jumped into another bush
And scratched them in again.

MORE MOTHER GOOSE
MELODIES

Dear Children:

And so you want more, do you, more jolly Mother Goose Rhymes? Well, you shall have them, for here are some of the very nicest jingles Mother Goose ever sang.

Of course you would like to know all about Little Betty Blue who lost her holiday shoe and the Three Little Kittens who lost their mittens and dear little Bobby Shaftoe. Well, they are all here and so are Mary and her little lamb and many other queer people from Mother Goose's happy village. They have come to tell you all about themselves and to make your beautiful book complete.

MORE MELODIES

Boys and girls come out to play,
The moon doth shine as bright as day,
Leave your supper and leave your
   sleep,
And meet your playfellows in the
   street;
Come with a whoop and come with a
   call,
And come with a good will, or not at all.
Up the ladder and down the wall,
A halfpenny roll will serve us all.
You find milk and I'll find flour,
And we'll have a pudding in half an
   hour.

Bobby Shaftoe's gone to sea,
Silver buckles on his knee;
He'll come back and marry me,
         Pretty Bobby Shaftoe.

Bobby Shaftoe's fat and fair,
Combing down his yellow hair,
He's my love forevermore,
         Pretty Bobby Shaftoe.

See-saw, sacradown,
Which is the way to London town?
One foot up, the other foot down,
That is the way to London town.

Ride a cock horse to Shrewsbury
   Cross,
To buy little Johnny a galloping horse.
It trots behind and it ambles before
And Johnny shall ride till he can ride
   no more.

What are little boys made of,
   made of?
What are little boys made of?
Snaps and snails and puppy dogs'
   tails;
And that's what little boys are made
   of, made of.

What are little girls made of, made of?
What are little girls made of?
Sugar and spice and all that's nice;
And that's what little girls are made
   of, made of.

Jog on, jog on, the footpath way,
   And merrily jump the style, boys;
A merry heart goes all the day,
   Your sad one tires in a mile, boys.

Johnny shall have a new bonnet,
   And Johnny shall go to the fair,
And Johnny shall have a blue ribbon
   To tie up his bonny brown hair.
And why may not I love Johnny?
   And why may not Johnny love me?
And why may not I love Johnny,
   As well as another body?

And here's a leg for a stocking,
   And here's a leg for a shoe,
And here's a kiss for his daddy,
   And two for his mammy, I trow.
And why may not I love Johnny?
   And why may not Johnny love me?
And why may not I love Johnny,
   As well as another body?

"Where are you going to, my pretty
    maid?"
"I'm going a-milking, sir," she said.
"May I go with you, my pretty
    maid?"
"You're kindly welcome, sir," she
    said.
"What is your father, my pretty
    maid?"
"My father's a farmer, sir," she
    said.
"What is your fortune, my pretty
    maid?"
"My face is my fortune, sir," she
    said.
"Then I can't marry you, my pretty
    maid!"
"Nobody asked you, sir!" she said.

Shoe the colt,
Shoe the colt,
Shoe the wild mare;
    Here a nail,
    There a nail,
Colt must go bare.

If wishes were horses,
    Beggars might ride;
If turnips were watches,
    I would wear one by my side.

Little girl, little girl, where have you
    been?
Gathering roses to give to the queen.
Little girl, little girl, what gave she
    you?
She gave me a diamond as big as my
    shoe.

For every evil under the sun,
There is a remedy, or there is none.
If there be one, try to find it;
If there be none, never mind it.

Little Tee Wee,
He went to sea
In an open boat;
And while afloat
The little boat bended,
And my story's ended.

Intery, mintery, cutery-corn,
Apple seed and apple thorn;
Wire, brier, limber-lock,
Five geese in a flock,
Sit and sing by a spring,
O-u-t, and in again.

I saw a ship a-sailing,
A-sailing on the sea;
And, oh! it was all laden
With pretty things for thee.

There were comfits in the cabin,
And apples in the hold;
The sails were all of silk,
And the masts were made of gold.

The four-and-twenty sailors
That stood between the decks,
Were four-and-twenty white mice
With chains about their necks.

The captain was a duck,
With a packet on his back;
And when the ship began to move,
The captain said, "Quack! quack!"

There was a little man,
And he had a little gun,
And his bullets were made of lead,
    lead, lead;
He went to the brook,
And saw a little duck,
And shot it through the head, head,
    head.

He carried it home
To his good wife Joan,
And bade her a fire to make, make,
    make;
To roast the little duck
He had shot in the brook,
And he'd go fetch the drake, drake,
    drake.

Hey, my kitten, my kitten.
And hey, my kitten, my deary,
Such a sweet pet as this
Was neither far nor neary.

Here we go up, up, up,
And here we go down, down,
    downy,
Here we go backward and forward,
And here we go round, round,
    roundy.

As Tommy Snooks and Bessie
    Brooks
Were walking out one Sunday;
Says Tommy Snooks to Bessie
    Brooks,
"To-morrow—will be Monday."

Three little kittens lost their mittens,
And they began to cry,
Oh! mother dear, we very much
    fear
That we have lost our mittens.
Lost your mittens! You naughty
    kittens!
Then you shall have no pie.
    Mee-ow, mee-ow, mee-ow.
No, you shall have no pie.
    Mee-ow, mee-ow, mee-ow.

The three little kittens found their
    mittens,
And they began to cry,
Oh! mother dear, see here, see
    here,
See, we have found our mittens.
Put on your mittens, you silly
    kittens,
And you may have some pie.
    Purr-r, purr-r, purr-r,
Oh! let us have the pie,
    Purr-r, purr-r, purr-r.

The three little kittens put on their
    mittens,
And soon ate up the pie;
Oh! mother dear, we greatly fear
That we have soiled our mittens.
Soiled your mittens! you naughty
    kittens!
Then they began to sigh,
    Mi-ow, mi-ow, mi-ow.
Then they began to sigh,
    Mi-ow, mi-ow, mi-ow.

The three little kittens washed their
    mittens,
    And hung them out to dry;
    Oh! mother dear, do you not hear,
    That we have washed our mittens.
Washed your mittens! Oh! you're
    good kittens.
    But I smell a rat close by.
        Hush! hush! mee-ow. mee-ow.
We smell a rat close by,
    Mee-ow, mee-ow, mee-ow.

Here sits the Lord Mayor,
    Here sits his two men,
Here sits the cock,
    Here sits the hen,
Here sits the little chickens,
    Here they run in,
Chin chopper, chin chopper,
    Chin chopper, chin!

Dance to your daddie,
    My bonnie laddie,
Dance to your daddie, my bonnie
    lamb!
    You shall get a fishie,
    On a little dishie,
You shall get a fishie when the boat
    comes hame.

Dance to your daddie,
    My bonnie laddie,
Dance to your daddie, and to your
    mammie sing!
    You shall get a coatie,
    And a pair of breekies,
You shall get a coatie when the boat
    comes in.

Diddlty, diddlty, dumpty,
The cat ran up the plum tree;
Give her a plum and down she'll
    come,
Diddlty, diddlty, dumpty.

Rock-a-bye baby,
Thy cradle is green;
Father's a nobleman,
Mother's a queen,
And Betty's a lady
And wears a gold ring,
And Johnny's a drummer
And drums for the king.

Little Betty Blue
Lost her holiday shoe.
What will poor Betty do?
Why, give her another
To match the other,
And then she will walk in two.

This is the way the ladies ride,
    Prim, prim, prim.
This is the way the gentlemen ride,
    Trim, trim, trim.
Presently come the country folks.
    Hobbledy gee, hobbledy gee

Clap, clap handies,
Mammie's wee, wee ain;
Clap, clap handies,
Daddie's comin' hame;
Hame till his bonny wee bit laddie;
Clap, clap handies,
My wee, wee ain.

Little Bo-peep has lost her sheep,
    And can't tell where to find them;
Leave them alone, and they'll come
        home,
    And bring their tails behind them.

Little Bo-peep fell fast asleep,
    And dreamt she heard them
        bleating;
But when she awoke, she found it a
        joke,
    For still they were all fleeting.

Then she took up her little crook,
    Determined for to find them;
She found them indeed, but it made
        her heart bleed,
    For they'd left their tails behind
        them.

✤

Smiling girls, rosy boys,
Come and buy my little toys,
Monkeys made of gingerbread,
And sugar horses painted red.

✤

Cock-a-doodle-doo!
My dame has lost her shoe;
My master's lost his fiddle stick
And knows not what to do.

✤

Pussy-cat Mole jumped over a coal,
And in her best petticoat burnt a
        great hole.
Poor pussy's weeping, she'll have
        no more milk
Until her best petticoat's mended
        with silk.

If all the world were apple pie,
    And all the sea were ink,
And all the trees were bread and
        cheese,
    What should we have to drink?

✤

My dear, do you know
How, a long time ago,
    Two poor little children,
Whose names I don't know,

Were stolen away
On a fine summer's day,
    And left in a wood,
As I've heard people say?

And when it was night,
So sad was their plight,
    The sun it went down,
And the moon gave no light!

They sobbed and they sighed,
And they bitterly cried,
    And the poor little things
They laid down and died.

And when they were dead,
The robins so red
    Brought strawberry leaves
And over them spread.

And all the day long
They sang them this song:
"Poor babes in the wood!
Poor babes in the wood!
    And don't you remember
The babes in the wood?"

A was an Apple pie;
   B bit it;
      C cut it;
         D dealt it;
            E ate it;
               F fought for it;

G got it;
   H had it;
      J joined it;
         K kept it;
            L longed for it;
               M mourned for it;

N nodded at it;
   O opened it;
      P peeped in it;
         Q quartered it;
            R ran for it;
               S stole it;

T took it;
   V viewed it;
      W wanted it;
         X, Y, Z, and ampers-and,
            All wished for a piece in
            hand.

✤

Monday's bairn is fair of face,
Tuesday's bairn is full of grace,
Wednesday's bairn is full of woe,
Thursday's bairn has far to go,
Friday's bairn is loving and giving,
Saturday's bairn works hard for its
   living;
But the bairn that is born on the
   Sabbath day
Is bonny and blithe and good and
   gay.

Ring-a-ring-a-roses,
A pocket full of posies;
Hush! hush! hush! hush!
We're all tumbled down.

✤

One, Two — buckle my shoe;
Three, Four — open the door;
Five, Six — pick up sticks;
Seven, Eight — lay them straight;
Nine, Ten — a good fat hen;
Eleven, Twelve — I hope you're well;
Thirteen, Fourteen — draw the
   curtain;
Fifteen, Sixteen — the maid's in the
   kitchen;
Seventeen, Eighteen — she's in
   waiting;
Nineteen, Twenty — my stomach's
   empty.

✤

A cat came fiddling out of a barn,
With a pair of bagpipes under her
   arm;
She could sing nothing but fiddle-
   de-dee,
The mouse has married the
   bumble-bee;
Pipe, cat — dance, mouse —
We'll have a wedding at our good
   house.

✤

Dickery, dickery, dare,
The pig flew up in the air;
The man in brown soon brought him
   down,
Dickery, dickery, dare.

Come when you're called,
Do what you're bid,
Shut the door after you,
Never be chid.

Elizabeth, Elspeth, Betsy and Bess,
They all went together to seek a
    bird's nest;
They found a bird's nest with five
    eggs in it,
They all took one and left four in it.

Hot-cross buns!
Hot-cross buns!
One a penny, two a penny,
Hot-cross buns!

If ye have no daughters,
Give them to your sons.
One a penny, two a penny,
Hot-cross buns!

If I'd as much money as I could
    spend,
I never would cry old chairs to mend,
Old chairs to mend, old chairs to
    mend;
I never would cry, old chairs to
    mend.

If I'd as much money as I could tell,
I never would cry old clothes to sell,
Old clothes to sell, old clothes to sell;
I never would cry, old clothes to sell.

Mary had a little lamb
    With fleece as white as snow,
And everywhere that Mary went
    The lamb was sure to go.

It followed her to school one day—
    That was against the rule.
It made the children laugh and play
    To see a lamb at school.

And so the teacher turned it out,
    But still it lingered near,
And waited patiently about
    Till Mary did appear.

"Why does the lamb love Mary so?"
    The eager children cry.
"Why, Mary loves the lamb, you
    know!"
    The teacher did reply.

Oh, I am so happy!
    A little girl said,
As she sprang like a lark
    From her low trundle bed.
It is morning, bright morning,
    Good morning, papa!
Oh, give me one kiss
    For good morning, mamma!

Cocks crow in the morn
    To tell us to rise,
And he who lies late
    Will never be wise;
For early to bed
    And early to rise
Is the way to be healthy,
    Wealthy and wise.

LIST OF ILLUSTRATIONS
(ARRANGED IN ORDER OF APPEARANCE)